D0960794

I only have two thoughts: One is *Run* and one is *Stay*.

IF I STAY under the car, I could get squished when it moves. But if I leave, who knows what I'll find out there?

And then I remember a city rule: Never stay anywhere if you can't see.

So I run, which is smart. Only I run into the street, which is not.

A big truck speeds toward me. Someone screams and I run to the left, away from the truck. I run between two cars. I run through a pair of legs. I run right through an open door.

I run up stairs. So many stairs! I don't count them. I just run and run and don't stop until I have to.

And then I'm on a roof.

HARVEY

AND THE COLLECTION OF IMPOSSIBLE THINGS

GARRET WEYR

Illustrations by MINNIE PHAN

chronicle books·san francisco

Library of Congress Cataloging-in-Publication Data available.

ISBN 978-1-7972-0690-5

Manufactured in China.

Design by Jennifer Tolo Pierce.
Typeset in Begum and Blaue Brush.

10 9 8 7 6 5 4 3 2 1

Chronicle Books LLC
680 Second Street
San Francisco, California 94107

Chronicle Books—we see things differently. Become part of our community at www.chroniclekids.com.

For Christine Marshall,
cat whisperer and bravest of souls.

PART ONE

OUT HERE

FOOD, GLORIOUS FOOD

IN THE CITY, hunger and danger chase you all day long. And you, if you are a city cat, chase food and safety. Every day, it's a race.

I am a city cat. Today hunger is winning. It's winning by a lot.

I'm very hungry.

I check all the usual spots for food starting with the garbage cans on 10th Street. There are already five big cats digging in them.

"No room for you," the cats growl. They do not want to share, and I do not want to fight.

Next, I check the bakery, which isn't far from these particular garbage cans. But I only catch food there when I'm lucky, so not today.

The train stations, busy, noisy, and stinky on most days, are so full of humans that I can't get close enough to the places where they might drop food.

Behind the restaurants where there's often food, all I see are shadows.

At every café table, there's a human in a bad mood. A human who says, *Go away, shoo, shoo.*

I'll have to find a dumpster. Dumpsters are where you can easily catch food, but where danger far more easily catches you if you are not prepared for a fight. I was born under a dumpster, in fact. A big one behind a restaurant.

In the city, that's a good place to be born. If you're a good fighter, it's safe and there's food nearby. Most city cats seek out dumpsters when they're hungry. Not me and here's why:

Dogs. Love. Dumpsters.

Most city cats make short work of dogs. Our nails are sharper and we're faster than they are. Even the fiercest dog is no match for a fierce cat. My mother, who was famous for her city cat ways, chased two dogs and three rats away from our dumpster before I was born. She was one of the best fighters the city ever had.

I'm not brave and fierce like my mother, but I am hungry. And hungry cats do desperate things.

Today, my belly is so empty and angry with hunger that I walk all the way uptown to a dumpster on the city hospital's north side. It is the least dangerous dumpster in the city. Partly because it's far away from the city's center, but mostly because the food you find there is terrible.

I smell it before I see it. Old coffee, Jell-O, and warm yogurt. Chipped, green, and uglier than ugly.

I take another smell, hoping there's something in it that's better than spoiled egg salad. Once, long ago, I ate the remains of an omelet with ham and cheese. It was from old Mrs. Gianni, who normally flicks a dish towel at me but sometimes gives me food.

The omelet made me picky about eggs. It was beyond magnificent.

I jump up on the dumpster and start to poke around for the spoiled egg salad. I move aside a crumpled coffee cup and some soggy fried

4

potatoes. And, then suddenly, I get a small whiff of a turkey sandwich. It's bliss and joy and, oh, glorious food! It's not just any old turkey sandwich, either, but one with a bit of cheese still attached.

This is the blessing of being a city cat: Everything is terrible until, just like that, it isn't.

But as I start to dig for the turkey, there's a rustle down in all the tossed-away things. A huge rat pokes his head out of the trash and shows me his teeth.

I jump back in surprise, feeling annoyed and scared right down to my paws. Those are sharp teeth.

"Beat it, Stripy," he says.

I have white lines that crisscross my gray fur. My brother, sister, and our mother sometimes called me Mr. Boots instead of Harvey because of the white fur on my paws. As nicknames go, I prefer Mr. Boots to Stripy.

"My name is Harvey," I say.

I try to say it with the pride and dignity our mother insisted all cats in the city have.

"We are simply the best," she'd tell my brother, sister, and me.

Maybe so, but it's hard to be proud (or dignified) when sitting on the edge of a dumpster full of the city's saddest garbage.

"I don't care what your name is," the rat says. "Get out."

I try not to look at his big, sharp teeth. I'm so hungry that I can still smell the turkey with cheese underneath the smell of my own fear. Fear has a smell like vinegar. It's sharp and demanding.

"That turkey is mine," the rat says, as if he can read my mind.

I haven't eaten anything in two days. That turkey is not his! A brave city cat would fight him for it. I think about my brother, whose nickname is The Terrific Thief. He's even more famous than my mother. What would he say to this rat?

"I have as much right to be here as you," I say.

But, of course, my brother wouldn't speak to a rat. He would chase it away.

"If you take one step further, I will bite you," the rat says.

He stares at me with his fiery eyes, big teeth, and twitchy nose.

My famous brother got his nickname because he stole an entire steak while the nearby humans were looking for matches. He jumped up on the rusty edge of the grill, sank his teeth into the meat, and took off.

I'm told he did not share it.

I'm not like my brother. I'm a city cat, yes. But not a brave one.

I do not take one step further. Instead, I jump off the dumpster and skitter back into the alley.

As I slink away, I try not to think about that turkey. I wish I were brave enough to fight a rat. My only defense is that he was really big.

Of course, I'm still hungry. And sad. Unlike turkey with cheese, hungry with sad is a terrible combination. I keep thinking about my empty belly and that huge rat until I remember to look up at the sky.

No matter how bad it gets, there's always the sky.

It's the best part of living in the city. During the day, the clouds say, *Go find food, you can do it*! And when it's dark out and the big, mean creatures are in big, mean moods, the silver stars say, *All is well, have no fear*.

Plus, sparrows swoop and fly through the sky. Of all the city's creatures, sparrows are the best. Unlike pigeons, who put humans in terrible moods, sparrows make everyone happy. And if you run into sparrows under a café table (and I almost always do), they only eat dropped bits of bread. They leave the real food for us.

I don't know any sparrows personally, but I like them. Most city cats hunt and eat sparrows, but not me. Who would want to chew through all those feathers? I'm so hungry today that I guess I wouldn't mind—but I'm never going to eat a sparrow. Even if they tasted like bacon, I wouldn't *eat* one. Not when they've always been so friendly.

My brother (who certainly does eat sparrows when he can't find other food), once said to me, *Harvey, you're not a real city cat. You're just a cat who's hungry most of the time and has no safe place of his own.* It wasn't very nice, but it's true.

Still, at least I'm not like the sad, poor creatures who live indoors. They sleep on beds and eat from delicate dishes. Yes, they are safe and always have food. But they can only dream about life under the sky.

I do not dream that dream because the sky and I share a life. I don't mind working hard to catch food and safety if it means I can live under the sky. But the sky, like the city, demands that you catch a third thing.

You can't live out here without catching luck. Without it, you won't live at all.

2

CITY HUNTING

I CATCH MOST of my luck at a bakery near the garbage cans on 10th Street. It isn't just its food that makes it lucky, but a woman in a blue shirt. Today, she comes out from the bakery's kitchen. She puts a dish on the ground. *Clink.*

Today's a lucky day.

The dish always has chicken and cheese. She always smells like vanilla and mint.

"Hello, Harvey."

I don't know how she knows my name, but she always says it. It's not the kind of thing humans know about city cats. I wish I knew hers. It's on my list of things to do:

1. Learn the name of the woman in blue shirt.

2. Save sister from jail.

3. Become a brave city cat.

4. Catch food.

5. Catch safety.

It's not a to-do list so much as a collection of impossible things. But when I eat chicken and cheese and listen to her say *Hello, Harvey,* everything seems possible.

Most city cats refuse to go anywhere near humans because they drive these shiny things they call *cars* that kill lots of us. For example, my mother was run over by a *bus,* which is a really big car, a few hours after we'd all left the dumpster.

She'd told us it was time for us to go out into the world and find our own way. We think she must have been tired after looking after us for so long. Tired enough that she forgot to pay attention and *SPLAT.*

If they don't yell at us or hit us with their shiny things, humans lock us up. My sister once looked for food *in* a restaurant instead of *behind* it. The chef caught her and sent her to the animal jail. Humans call it a *shelter*, but we all know better. Shelter keeps you dry and safe. Jail has cages and lots of animals locked up.

No one has seen my sister since she went in there. That's why she's on my list.

Humans will say *Go away, shoo shoo* but they will also give you food. I never know who is going to do which. Except with the woman in the blue shirt. If I find her, she always gives me food.

When I'm done eating, she takes the dish away.

"See you next time, Harvey," she says. "You be safe."

She says that as if I could just choose to be safe. Safety is harder to catch than food. But I can feel the rain coming (the air smells soft) so she's right: I need to find my place to stay safe and dry during the storm. Otherwise, rain will make my fur heavy and cold.

With my full belly, I hunt safety. In the city, confusing humans, cranky cats, and crankier dogs hog all the best spots. Still, you have to look. Without safety you will wind up *SPLAT* on the street. And who wants that?

I don't.

The places where I normally look are under park benches, behind museums, or in courtyards. On rainy or snowy days, benches are no good. And courtyards only work if you can sneak under a window box with no one noticing. Mrs. Gianni has the one window box in the city that no other cat has claimed. But she's in a bad mood and flicks her towel at anyone before they even get close. Her window box has strong-smelling herbs and small red flowers. She doesn't like a *nasty cat* near her plants. It's why no one owns that spot. Her towel is dangerous.

I'm anxious about the rain and investigate my emergency places where I sometimes find shelter. The park behind the library has a small shop with a little porch that's dry and quiet. Once or twice, I've hidden there during a bad storm.

But not today. Today, a skinny dog runs out from under the porch. Another skinny dog pokes his nose out and yells at him, "This is my place!"

I turn around and head over to the Mayor's mansion by the East River. It's forty streets away with lots of cars and buses to avoid, but it must be done. It takes a while, but I get there. I slip through the gate to search the spots in the garden that will keep you dry.

"Kitty!" It's the mayor's granddaughter. She runs toward me. "My kitty!"

She picks me up and tries to hug me. It's awful. Human girls are either quietly pleasant or loudly full of hugs.

Cats. Do. Not. Like. Hugs.

I try to get away by squirming. I squirm carefully because she's pulled my ears more than once. I could scratch her, but why scratch a silly girl?

"Kitty, my kitty!" she keeps saying.

The mayor's guards with their heavy boots and big voices run toward us.

"Get out of here, fleabag," one of them says.

"Go on, go," says the other. "Go now."

That is how guards say *Go away, shoo shoo.* The girl drops me and I run out the gate.

There's one more place where I sometimes catch safety. I walk along the buildings on 84th Street until I get to the park. Right by the city's biggest park is the city's biggest museum. And behind that museum is the city's biggest drainpipe. No one bothers you there and it's dry. It's my favorite place, but it's not my place. It's Chester's place. And Chester is a dog.

CHESTER'S PAWS

NOT JUST ANY dog, but one of the fiercest dogs in the city. I'm not afraid of him because he's the kind of fierce that doesn't fight with small creatures. Dogs like this are rare. He's actually the only one I know.

We first met right under his drainpipe on a snowy day. I was so happy I'd found a dry place that even though it smelled like a dog, I curled up and fell asleep. When Chester returned, he waited until I woke up and said, "Ahoy, there, my small friend. This is my place, but you're always welcome to use it if I'm not here."

Today I'm hoping that he might be out and about as he doesn't mind the rain. Dogs are strange that way.

As I turn the corner toward the drainpipe, I see Chester's big brown paws. And the profile of a medium-sized gray dog who's listening to a stern lecture.

"If I hear from one more squirrel that you are chasing them for the fun of it, I am going to be very angry," Chester says. "What have I told you about them?"

"Squirrels have as much right to the park as we do," the gray dog says.

"What else?"

"To save my energy for food catching," the dog says. "Sorry, Chester."

He is hanging his head down and sounds embarrassed.

"That's okay, I know it's hard," Chester says. "But before you go, one more thing: Your place behind the hotel is big enough for you to share with at least one other dog. I heard you made an old dog leave. You find her and invite her back."

The other dog mumbles something. I realize I can't hide from the rain here. Chester's lectures can last a long time. I'd better go look in the nearest train station. They are the worst places in the city and smell like wet laundry and pee. Also, they're full of light, noise, and busy people who hate cats. I only go in them when I'm desperate.

The rain starts sending down its drops. I cough through my nose. *Ah-choo-ooo.* Chester turns his head at the sound of my sneeze and thumps his tail when he sees me.

"Ahoy, my young friend," he says. "Need shelter from the rain?"

"No, no," I say, watching carefully as the gray dog walks past me, head still down and tail between his legs. "I'm just on my way to the 86th Street station."

"You stay here," Chester says. "I'll move over a squidge so we can both sit."

In truth, I like that better than being here alone. Chester is warm, and you're always safe with him because he's a good fighter. A year ago, I saw him defend his spot from another dog. That dog was stronger than strong and refused to move even when Chester growled and showed his teeth.

In the end, there was snarling and blood, but it wasn't Chester's, thank goodness. The other dog ran off and Chester got his place back. When he saw me hiding in the museum's shadow, he laughed.

"Everything's okay," he said. "That dog just didn't know how to share, and places should always be shared."

"At least you have a place to share," I told him. "And defend."

"Harvey, you keep looking for a place," Chester always tells me. "You'll find one, I promise."

I keep looking but nothing yet. Most places in the city have been taken by city creatures who are bigger or fiercer than I am. To get a place in the city, you have to fight for it. Chester thinks everyone should share their places, but even though he can order some creatures to do that, he can't order them all.

I wish he could because I'm no good at fighting.

But today, I don't have to fight because I'm with Chester. The rain changes from drops to rivers and then into the worst kind of rain: hail.

I watch the sharp little balls of angry water shooting down from the sky. A few of them hit me on the side, exploding into my fur with heavy wet yuck.

"Summer storms are the worst," Chester says. "Get between my paws and tuck up under my head."

I put my head against one paw and curl my tail against the other. We listen to the angry balls of water bounce off the drainpipe. I can feel Chester moving with his breath. I'm dry and warm. It's the coziest, nicest place I've been since the last time I was here.

Slowly the hail turns back to rivers and then drops. The sun spreads softly against the sky. The drops stop. No more rain. We both stretch.

"I'm glad you're here," Chester says, "But if you tell anyone I let you touch my paws, I'll have to eat you."

He laughs to show me he is partly teasing, but only partly. I understand why. A city dog only rules if other dogs are afraid of him. Chester has been alive for a long time and he knows the tricks for surviving better than I do. In addition to having his own spot, he's excellent at finding food. Hunger and danger almost never catch him.

But Chester once lived with a human, so he has a bad habit, one that none of us can afford: Chester gets attached to things other than the sky. I've seen him give food to older, weak dogs. He knows which humans to stay away from, and which ones will give food and ear rubs.

And he's very kind to me, which is a lucky thing. For me, but maybe not for him.

The Terrific Thief says only the weak care about anything other than luck and the sky. If you care, he says, it distracts you from fighting for what's yours. You will get tired from worrying about another creature and make a mistake. The way our mother did. And, my brother says, you must never ever let a human touch you.

All the same, I think Chester knows how to be fierce *and* attached. He certainly gives plenty of good advice.

Things like, *Don't go way downtown. There are too many taxis there.* And, *Park benches are good spots for safety if it's not raining.* Also, *Never forget what you can do, Harvey.*

When I don't catch food or when danger catches me, I say, *Harvey, you can do this.* It reminds me of Chester. It makes me believe I can catch food and safety. Hunting for them is hard work, but also the best work.

Chester leaves for the park to make his rounds and says I can stay. I curl my tail around myself and add one more impossible thing to my collection:

6. Repay Chester for his kindness.

How to do that is a question that stalks me through the city like a new hunger.

STAIRS

WHACK.

The whole world shakes and my eyes see black and silver. When I can see again, I jump back and yell, "Newspapers are for reading!"

Of course, all the conductor hears is *Meow, meowrr meow*. I eye a piece of steak that's fallen from his sandwich. Just then, a rat darts out and grabs the steak. *NO FAIR! I SAW IT FIRST!*

Of course, *grabbing* first is what matters. And that goes double in a train station. It's why I only come here when I'm desperate. And today is another desperate day. The city will give you lots of them.

"Go away, shoo shoo," the conductor says.

When I get outside, I look up at the sky and for just a moment I forget how hungry I am. But there's no time for the sky today. Food is the only thing I have time for.

I go to three cafés, and at each one, the waiters throw something; a fork (it misses), water (it gets on my feet!), and a bread roll. It bounces off my head and then lands in the gutter where an ugly, noisy pigeon swoops down to grab it.

In the city, you always have to hope for luck. But on really bad days, even luck fails.

So, of course, the woman in the blue shirt is not at the bakery. I try to pick up her smell and follow it, but get confused. I wind up in a neighborhood that doesn't have restaurants or cafés. It's near the park, where it's hard to catch food without also catching danger.

I find a courtyard that's quiet enough that I can finally rest. I try to think of places to look for food where no one will be yelling or throwing, when I see there's a boy in a doorway looking at me. I look back.

Of all humans, boys can be the most dangerous. Or the nicest. It's strange, but true. This boy does not throw anything or yell. Good, I think.

He goes inside and comes back out with a dish. It smells like fish. I LOVE fish. It is my favorite. I hope the boy will drop some.

Instead he puts the dish on the ground. I look at it and then back at the boy. He kicks it toward me. It makes a loud sound: *kadunk*. The dish smells so very good. It smells like happiness itself.

The dish isn't that far away. I wait to see if the boy moves. He doesn't.

I'm hungry, so I step forward, one step at a time. I move slowly until my nose is right by the dish. Have I mentioned that I love fish? It's rich and soft, but also filling. I take bite after bite of all that rich, soft, and filling fish. I'm not paying attention to anything else.

Suddenly, the world is upside down! I'm swinging through the air!

The dish is below me and the boy holds my tail. It hurts. It hurts a lot! He's too far away to scratch so I *mmmrrrooowww* at him. He drops me, and I run.

I run away from humans all the time. It's what you do if someone whaps you with a newspaper or throws things at you or yells, *Go away, shoo, shoo.*

But this time, the boy chases me down the street. No human has ever chased me before. I don't like it. I run fast, but the boy shouts and throws stones. I don't like that either.

I run under a car and for a minute, I think I'm safe. I stand and pant. Hiding under cars is not smart.

Everyone knows that. It might start moving and then you are *SPLAT*.

A stick snakes under the car. It's long and sharp. I know the boy is at the other end. He pokes it all over. It almost hits me.

If I run out, he will come after me with that stick. If I stay, he will hit me with that stick. I can't think. I try to say, *Harvey, you can do this,* but I don't know what to do.

My heart beats a *thump thump whoosh* sound into my ears. It means, *This is the worst day of your life. Thump thump whoosh.* It also means, *You're probably going to die.*

I don't want to die. At all. I want to save myself, but how?

It's very hard to think when your heart beats out the alarm that you're going to die. I only have two thoughts: One is *Run* and one is *Stay.* They are not helpful thoughts.

Then a voice shouts at the boy: "Stop that! Right now, right this minute!"

The voice is strict and gentle at the same time. There's a scraping sound and a yelp. The stick vanishes. I can't see if the boy and the stick are still there waiting for me.

If I stay under the car, I could get squished when it moves. But if I leave, who knows what I'll find out there?

And then I remember a city rule: Never stay any-where if you can't see.

So I run, which is smart. Only I run into the street, which is not.

A big truck speeds toward me. Someone screams and I run to the left, away from the truck. I run between two cars. I run through a pair of legs. I run right through an open door.

I run up stairs. So many stairs! I don't count them. I just run and run and don't stop until I have to.

I'm on a roof.

I've never been on one before. They are normally things you see, but don't think about. In my life, I've seen so many roofs high up in the sky.

Now I'm on one, which is strange and unexpected, but far less scary than where I was. I stand at the edge of the roof and pant for breath. There's a water tower on one side and under it, some shade. The shade will be a dry space if it rains. In the middle of the roof there's a circle of orange pots with dark dirt, fat bushes, and flowers.

The smell of vanilla and mint hangs over those pots.

I walk slowly around the edges, sniff in each corner, and then look out in the direction of the park. Even though it's a very big park, it seems small from here. I am far away from every danger that lives down in the city.

Thump thump whoosh fades away. And in its place, my heart beats *whooo* in my ears. That means *I am never leaving here.*

But I'll have to go and look for food, I tell the sound. It's been two days with basically no food. A cat can only be hungry for so long before it dies.

Whooo beats my heart in my ears. *I am never leaving.*

I'm too tired to argue.

Someone comes through the door and I freeze with terror. My legs get ready to run back down the stairs when I smell fish. Is it the boy again? But instead of a *kadunk,* there's only a quiet *clink.*

"Hello," says a voice.

It's soft and gentle, but also the voice from the bakery, which is strange. A roof is not a bakery. I turn away from the ledge to look at the human.

It's the woman in the blue shirt.

"That was brave of you to run up the stairs," she says, kneeling by a dish of fish scraps.

I tilt my head and look at her. The worst part about humans is that I can understand every word they say.

But when I speak, all they hear is gibberish. Maybe this is why we city creatures find humans so confusing. We can't tell them what we want.

I can't tell her I ran up the stairs because I was terrified, not brave.

I can't explain that I had no choice.

I can't even ask for her name.

Which suddenly seems like the most important item on my list and something I should have found out before now.

Mostly though, I want that fish and think it's for me, but nothing is for certain way up here.

As she looks at me, I can't decide if I should approach her or back up. She's lucky at the bakery, but humans are mostly dangerous. Here on the roof, which one is she?

PART TWO

UP HERE

5

IMPOSSIBLY POSSIBLE

SHE CLUCKS SOFTLY. *Kuh, tuk, kuk.* In a day full of yelling humans, screeching tires, and *thump thump whoosh,* it's the first nice sound I've heard.

"You eat," she says. "I'm sorry it's not cheese."

She leaves the roof. I walk slowly to the dish, worried it's another trick. But hunger beats out worry and I put my tongue in the bowl.

Fish washes across my tongue and dances through my body. The sheer relief of eating rushes into every corner of me—even my paws and ears. With each bite, the desperate day fades away.

Soon I am licking the edges of the bowl and my belly is full of *thank you.*

Clink. The woman in the blue shirt is back with a dish of water. She moves away and sits down.

"You're safe now, Harvey," she says.

She sits quietly with me for a long while. It's like being behind the bakery but better. She isn't getting up and telling me to be safe. I'm not worrying about where to go next. When she does get up, she does it slowly and quietly.

"I love the city from up here," she says. "I hope I see you tomorrow, but I'll keep the door to the stairs open. Just in case you want to leave."

I don't.

For the first time in a very long time, I end the day with a full belly and no worry about where I'll sleep.

ᘓ

The woman in the blue shirt comes every day with food. Every day I ask for her name, thank her for the food, and say that I'm delighted to see her. She always smiles and says *Kuh, tuk, kuk.*

One day, just as I am asking her name, she laughs gently.

"You're a talkative one," she says. "At the bakery, you never said a thing."

"Well, I was too hungry to chat," I tell her.

"It's nice for me to know you're here," she says. "When I'm at work, I think about you. I imagine that you look out for the plants."

She *loves* her plants. After she brings my food, she often stays to take care of them. She even talks to them! I think she knows that plants don't talk, but maybe she understands their silence. After all, she knows my name.

When she is not on the roof, I tell the plants that I am here to look out for them.

"Let me know if you need anything," I say.

So far, none of them have answered. I do not use them as the bathroom, which is how most of us use plants down below. On my first day here, the woman in the blue shirt put dirt and sand in a box for me to use.

I've never had my own bathroom before, but I like it.

Every morning, I wake up without worrying about food. I don't have to catch safety. It's right here on the roof. Hunger and danger no longer chase me.

It's odd that when I ran away from the boy—ran faster than I ever have—and was more afraid than I'd ever been, I checked two items off my list: I'm safe and I'm never hungry.

That's the city—everything changes in the oddest ways.

Of course, I'm never going to become a brave city cat up here. Or repay Chester or save my sister from prison. That's what keeps the list impossible. But here, it doesn't matter.

Here, I have time for what *is* possible.

The sun still sets every day, bringing cooler air and the dark silvery sky. And it's back up again in the morning. But somehow, the days are longer. Up here, there's no schedule.

The woman in the blue shirt comes in the morning with food. Sometimes she sits with me, but not always. Sometimes she waters and talks to her plants and sometimes she doesn't. In the evening, she brings me more food and then leaves. She might bring the evening food before the sun goes down or after it has already set.

Nothing here is like life in the city. There's no running around to stay alive. I have time for things I didn't even know needed time.

For example, each and every day, the sky and I have a proper greeting. I study all the ways it's blue. From up here, the sky and the sun fill the city with shadows and light.

At first, my days seem strangely empty. Even if the woman in the blue shirt sits with me while I eat and talks to her plants, I have so much time! So. Much. Time.

But slowly, I notice how food and safety grow to fill my days as much as fear and hunger ever did.

I have a nap after I greet the sky. I nap after I eat and also after I check on the plants. I even nap after I look out across the city.

No city cat, even the bravest of the brave, naps. You can't nap if you chase food and safety. You certainly can't nap if hunger and danger chase you. But you *can* nap if you live on this roof.

Naps are like lots of shade and cool water on a hot day.

❧

One evening, after bringing my food, the woman in the blue shirt returns with a cup. It has blue and purple flowers painted on it. She sits down next to the orange pots and looks at me.

The sun has already set, and the sky is the light gray it gets before going black and silver. When she brought the food, the sky was still a light blue. Normally, she only ever sits when she brings my food in the morning.

"*Kuh, tuk, kuk,*" she says. "I thought I'd have my tea with you."

Steam floats up from her cup like a wisp of fog.

"That's so pretty," I tell her. "It looks like the end of a rainy day is caught in your cup."

"I love your 'meow,'" she says. "It's one of my two favorite sounds."

"What's the other one?" I ask. "Also, what is your name?"

After all, learning hers should be the most possible part of life up here.

"At the bakery, when the oven dings, I am the first one there to open it," she says.

I know she's not really talking to me because she's looking around. When she talks to me, she looks right at me, so it feels like she understands me. Even though I know she doesn't.

"There's a sound that the oven makes," she says. "Everything is so quiet and perfect."

I want to tell her that the sound she makes when she says *kuh, tuk, kuk* is quiet and perfect. It's *my* favorite sound. But I stay quiet because I've already said enough.

She drinks her tea. I watch the steam fade away. Together, we are quiet and perfect. But mornings are a lot LESS quiet.

Only not because of us.

6

THE FAVORITE

WHEN SHE COMES in the morning, I eat while she sits to drink her coffee. Or, she puts down my food with a *clink* and says, "Harvey, I must dash. I'm late." Because we are high up, the sounds of the city waking are a low hum.

We should have lots of quiet in the mornings.

But sadly, pigeons are also here, high above the city. They are as noisy and annoying on the roof as they are down below. The woman in the blue shirt doesn't like them. No one who lives in the city does.

One morning, two especially large and loud pigeons fly around the water tower, yelling and screeching. They are having one of those annoying conversations that pigeons have.

"You did!" says one.

"Did not!" says the other. "You did."

"They are the worst," the woman in the blue shirt says, frowning at them. "At least they don't actually land on the roof anymore."

"No, you did!"

"Did not!"

"Before you came here, some of them even pooped on the plants," she says. "But you scared them away."

Me? I have never in my entire life scared anything. Maybe, without even trying, I've scared the pigeons enough so that they don't land? I watch them as they swoop and screech.

If I *tried* to scare them, would I be able to make them fly away completely?

I look at the woman in the blue shirt and then at the pigeons. They are much bigger than sparrows. In fact, they are about as big as a normal-sized rat.

If you don't look at their strange pink feet, there is nothing scary about them. Both of them are gray with bits of black here and there. One has green, shiny feathers all around his neck. They are just birds. They don't bite or scratch.

I remember an angry cat who chased me away from a garbage can. He hissed and snarled. I was so hungry that day that even when he showed his teeth, I tried to grab a bite of chicken pie before running away. It was a big mistake.

He scratched the top of my head and the scar still itches.

Hopefully, a cat has yelled at these pigeons before. Hopefully, they will be afraid of my teeth. Hopefully, I will not have to scratch them.

I walk over to the water tower. "Listen to me!"

The pigeons keep yelling "Did!" and "Did not!"

I try again. "You are not welcome anywhere near this roof!"

And then, for good measure, I pin my ears back and snarl. *Mmmrrrooowww.*

It works! They stop screeching at each other. They stop swooping. They flap in place.

"Let's go," one of them says.

The other one has already started to fly away.

"That was your fault," I hear it call out.

The other one swoops behind it. "No, yours!"

They're gone.

"My brave kitty," says the woman in the blue shirt.

"That was not brave," I tell her. Brave is a fight with another creature who has what you want or need. Brave is the most impossible item on my list. It has nothing to do with ugly, noisy birds.

"That was splendid, Harvey," she says. "Thank you."

I look around the roof at the plants and the water tower. No pigeons. Not one pigeon ever comes back. And she's right; that is pretty splendid.

ω

Summer ends and autumn begins. I almost don't notice because my food stays the same. It's always chicken with cheese, or fish bits. Down in the city, you catch different types of food depending on the seasons.

People will eat cold steak sandwiches or tuna salad in the summer. When winter is on its way, people eat chicken pie or fish stew. Once winter arrives, they have roast beef or spaghetti with meat sauce. And then in the spring they have broiled fish or ham.

If you are a city cat, you try to get as much of what is thrown away as possible.

But up here with the woman in the blue shirt, the food is the same no matter the season. It's delicious and it's mine.

And I eat it while she sits with me, which is the best part of all. Especially at night, when she comes back from the bakery and drinks her tea. Before she leaves, she will sometimes say, "I wish you'd come downstairs with me. You'd be safer and we'd have so much fun."

"But I'm a city cat," I always tell her. "Not a brave one, maybe, but a city one. We don't live with humans."

Three times, she has reached out her hand as if to pet me. Three times I've backed up away from her. The first time, I was so surprised that I pinned my ears back and my fur stood up. But she is a respectful human and, after the third failed attempt, no longer tries to pet me.

Instead, she sits and either we are quiet together or she talks about what happened that day. How the sugar buns got burned and they had to make honey buns instead. How there was a line all the way out the door for chocolate raspberry cakes.

"So many people love that cake," she says. "It's always a crowd favorite. But next week, I'll make an almond-cherry torte."

She went to Italy to learn how to make that. To Austria to learn to make the chocolate raspberry cake. To India to learn about mango-vanilla custard. The woman in the blue shirt is full of stories about food, far-away places, and the bakery on 10th Street. But she is not full of news about the city. Nor does she tell me her name.

I want to know about Chester, if the train stations are still stinky, and which dumpster is currently the most popular (or the most dangerous). Even though I've caught food and safety, I still want to hear all the news about the race everyone is running down below.

So, I have no choice but to invite three sparrows to land on the roof's edge.

THREE, THREE, THREE

AFTER ALL, YOU cannot get news by wishing for it. I first see them on top of the water tower. They are hopping around from foot to foot.

"I don't like it up here," says one of them. "An owl could get us."

"It's only for a moment," says the second one. "We have to rest."

"Ahoy, there," I say, trying to sound like Chester. "You're welcome here on the roof. I will protect you from owls."

That is an easy promise as everyone knows that owls never stray too far from trees in the park. Everyone except the sparrows, I guess. Of course, they have bird-brains.

"You're a cat," the first one says. "You'll eat us."

"I'm not that kind of cat," I say.

"I know you!" says the second. "I met you under a café table once. You were hiding from a big cat. I like you."

The third one is quiet.

They fly down from the water tower and sit on the roof's ledge.

"You can come here whenever you want," I tell them. "To rest or have a chat. And have no fear, I do not eat birds."

They introduce themselves. Or rather, Flippy and Mippy do.

Flippy points a wing at the quiet sparrow and says, "That's Kippy."

I nod at Kippy, who jumps behind Mippy.

Flippy, Mippy, and Kippy fly here, there, and everywhere. Whatever happens down in the city, they know it. And they talk about it with each other in their chattering-sparrow way. Within days, I know all the news. The sparrows are how I keep up with everything down below.

Flippy is their leader. "Harvey, hello, hello," she says, as they fly to the roof.

"Yes, yes," Mippy says, when they land. "Yes, yes, yes."

Kippy never speaks to me. Instead, he watches me very carefully. He looks as if he's busy solving all of the world's problems. But also as if he's worried that I might eat him.

I understand what it is to be afraid. I always say, "Hello, Kippy. Good of you to come."

I ask if they talk to Chester. I want to know how he is. But they can't tell me.

"We see him," Flippy explains. "But he is usually scolding another dog and barks at us not to get close."

I laugh. That sounds like Chester.

One morning, the sparrows arrive with news that's just for me.

"Your sister lives inside where we can see her," Flippy says. "A human went to the animal jail and adopted her. Now she lives in an apartment in a brick building."

"Yes, yes, yes," says Mippy. "She sits in the window and meows all day long."

"But at night she sits near her human on the couch," says Flippy. "And eats wet food."

What on earth is wet food? It sounds disgusting. My poor sister is trapped without any sky. I change number two on my collection of impossible things. *Save sister from*

jail is now *Save sister from brick cage.* Of course, to do that, I would have to leave the roof.

I'm not leaving. All my food and safety are here.

"I've often wondered why more cats don't live up over the city like we do," Flippy says. "It's so dangerous to live on the ground."

"Dogs and cats shouldn't live on the street," Mippy says. "They should all find a roof like Harvey did."

"Harvey found a human," Kippy says. "For a cat, a roof without a human is just the top of a building. It's not a place. It's not even safe."

I am so surprised to hear Kippy speak that I hardly hear Mippy say, "True, true, true."

"No food on the roof," says Flippy. "Not unless you have a human. Humans are the worst, but also the best."

"True, true, true."

"I don't have a human," I remind them. "I only have the sky."

I feel sad saying this, thinking of all the times she has asked me to come live with her. Even though I still haven't found a way to learn her name, sitting with her has been the best part of every day.

"You have the woman in the blue shirt," Flippy says.

"You do!" says Mippy. "Do, do, do."

You can't be a city cat and have a human. I'm not even sure if you can have a roof. But city creatures do have the sky. And the air it sends down, which begins to get colder.

8

SMALL, STRANGE THINGS

THE DAYS BEGIN to get short and the nights a little darker. The woman in the blue shirt comes to the roof with a box. The box has a door like a cage. Inside the box there is a blanket.

"Harvey, I really want you to come downstairs with me," she says. "It's going to get very cold. My apartment is warm and safe."

"No," I say.

"I got you this," she says and holds out the box. "I don't have to touch you. You just get in it and I'll carry the box to my apartment."

I like her, but I'm not going anywhere in a box with a door that looks like a cage. And I'm never going to an apartment, which is a human word for brick jail. She puts down the box. I hiss at it.

She looks behind her. "What's wrong?"

She puts her hand inside the cage and clucks. *Kuh, tuk, kuk.* I am not fooled and back away. I look at the ledge, but it's pointless. I already know that if I try to jump from my roof to the next roof, I will fall to the ground and be *SPLAT*. That's not an escape. That's death.

"Okay," she says. "I understand."

She takes off the door that looks like a cage.

"I'll leave the box here," she says. "That way you will be warm when it's cold."

She seems worried about the cold, but I am not. Maybe she doesn't know that winter is just one part of the year.

I never go in the box when she is around. But on the coldest nights, I sleep in it.

The blanket inside is soft and dry. The wind still blows through the box. And sometimes the snow drifts in. But mostly, it's warm enough. It's the first winter that cold doesn't catch me. I like the box but am glad no one can see me. A warm cage is the last place a fierce city creature would ever sleep.

ɷ

When soft air returns to the city and I can tell in my bones that the cold is gone, the woman in the blue shirt is busy. She brings up a new pot, a bag of dirt, and three small plants.

She sits on the ground and puts dirt in the new pot and makes three holes.

I roll in the dirt that spills out of the bag. I've never rolled in any kind of dirt before. It's fantastic! After I'm done with that, I sit down next to her and make myself clean. I notice how she smells like vanilla and mint but also dirt. And just a little bit like the fish she brings me.

It's a nice smell. I should smell like that, I think. I rub up against the smell.

"Why, Harvey," she says. "That's the first time you've touched me."

I don't say anything because I am as surprised as she is. But I don't walk away or back up. In fact, without thinking AT ALL, I press my head against her hand. She slowly opens her fingers and scratches my ears.

My throat makes the strangest sound! It's what a train would sound like if it were small and quiet. I've made it before, but only when eating after a long time of not eating. Her fingers rub into all the itchy spots. A

warm, pleasant feeling spreads through me, right down to the pads on my toes. *Hhhhmmm.*

This is better than every nap, every bowl of fish, and every minute spent with Chester. This is as good as being with my brother, my sister, and our mother under the dumpster.

"Harvey, you're the best," the woman in the blue shirt says.

All through the first part of summer, when the sun feels gentle and the new plants grow so quickly, I make sure that we touch. It's like catching safety.

"I love this time of year," she says. "Everything is possible."

She goes back to her books and magazines.

"That is true all the time," I tell her. "You can meet the meanest boy and the best human all on the same day."

But she doesn't listen, just keeps reading. She has books about Poland and magazines full of recipes for a Polish dessert. Paczki. She says it's pronounced POONCH-key.

If rolling around in warm dirt had a sound, the sound would be *POONCH-key.* Saying it makes me happy.

"Before I had the bakery, I traveled so often and learned new ways to make cakes and cookies," she says. "Now I can only go away once a year."

"What's your name?" I ask her. "You travel to the roof every day to feed me, I should know your name."

"You're so sweet, Harvey," she says. "If you were a person, I would learn to make POONCH-keys just for you."

"That's nice," I say.

And it is, but I wish she would tell me her name. She turns a page of her magazine. I look over her shoulder at pictures of the POONCH-keys.

"They're like donuts, but totally different," she tells me. "They have more butter and egg, so they're much yummier. And they're stuffed with the most amazing things."

One day, before my life on the roof, I was so hungry that I ate part of a sticky sweet bread with bits of red jam and powdered sugar on it. Someone had dropped it when hurrying out of a train station. I found out later that it was called a jelly donut.

Cats don't like jelly donuts. But maybe we like POONCH-keys?

"There's a place in Poland where they teach you how to make them," she says. "If I could go, we'd sell them at the bakery."

"Is there a roof for us in Poland?" I ask and press my head against her hand. "You won't leave me, right?"

RED

FLIPPY, MIPPY, AND Kippy report that the city's humans are doing what they do every summer. They are putting big bags in cars, locking their houses, and leaving the city for a period of time.

It's called a holiday. I guess if you don't live under the sky but are trapped inside, you sometimes need to go away. Even the woman in the blue shirt is going.

"I'll be in Poland!"

She shows me photographs of the hotel where she'll stay, and the small building where she'll learn to make POONCH-keys. It's in Kraków.

"Kraków sounds like *meow*," I tell her and we both laugh.

"You're not to worry, Harvey," she says. "I'll miss you, but I'll be back." I'm excited for her because she's so happy.

Then she brings another human to the roof. I haven't seen another human in such a long time that even if this human were a gentle, quiet one, it would be a shock. But she is not at all quiet. She has a loud voice, bright red pants, and very dark hair.

"Harvey, this is my friend Rachel," says the woman in the blue shirt.

"This is the cat you feed?" Rachel asks. "Mighty funny looking."

I run behind the box that has no door.

"He's beautiful," the woman in the blue shirt says. "If you knew anything about cats, you would see that."

Rachel laughs. Her laugh sounds like hail hitting Chester's drainpipe.

"Rachel will take care of you when I'm away," the woman in the blue shirt says to me.

Now I know the name of a human I never want to see again. But *not* the name of the one human whose name I *do* want to know.

Rachel kneels down. She puts her face much too close to mine. "Hello, Harvey."

She says it VERY LOUDLY. Maybe she thinks cats are deaf. We are not.

When the woman in the blue shirt and Rachel leave the roof, I try to understand how I can touch one human but be so afraid of the other one that I run away from her. It's true that some humans are good (they give you food) and some are terrible (they chase you down the street with a big stick). But there must be a way to know why that is. And which human is which.

I was always confused by Mrs. Gianni who was mean a lot of the time, but not always. The boy who chased me seemed safe until he grabbed my tail. Should I have known what he was going to do? The brave city creatures who fight for their places probably would have known.

Chester, who is the bravest of the brave, always knows right away about humans. He could teach me how to tell good humans from bad.

I can see the museum from here. I walk to the open door of the roof and look down the stairs. In order to talk to Chester, I'd have to go down all those stairs and then walk across the park to get there.

Nope.

I'm afraid of this Rachel and my roof has no hiding place. Still, I'm much more afraid of going back down to where there are boys, sticks, and humans who throw things.

What to do when the Rachel-human comes back? What if she's careless enough to step on my paw? Or hurt my ears with her loud voice? She might even lift me up by the tail.

I pace and swish. And then swish and pace. And then I know what to do.

ↄↄ

In the morning, when Rachel comes with fish and water, I'm already up on the tower's wide, smooth top. I can see out across the entire city *and* down onto the roof. I watch Rachel look for me everywhere. She even lifts the pots, which is not very smart of her. Does she really think I would fit under a pot?

Finally, she looks up.

"Gracious," she says in her annoyingly loud voice. "That's unexpected."

Then she laughs her big, sharp laugh. My roof is no place to be reminded of a wet, summer storm full of sharp, angry hail hitting the drainpipe.

Rachel waters the plants and leaves. After about an hour—to make sure she is not hiding by the steps and waiting to play a trick—I climb down and eat. And then I climb back up. It's nice up here. I like it.

The next day, after Rachel leaves, I sniff the pots. They don't smell like vanilla and mint anymore. Now, they smell like cinnamon and oranges.

I don't like that, so I climb back to the top of the tower.

When Flippy, Mippy, and Kippy arrive to rest and chat on the ledge, they are surprised. Flippy and Mippy fly up and land on the tower, but Kippy doesn't. He flits back and forth above them. He never wants to be that close to me.

"Why are you all the way up here?" Flippy asks. "You live on the roof, not the tower."

"Yes, yes, yes," Mippy says.

I explain that the human who brings my food is away and the one who has taken her place has red pants and is loud.

"She's also a little scary," I say. "The woman in the blue shirt is not scary. I need to know why some humans are terrible, some are good, and how to tell which is which."

I'm sure my mother knew. But she was so busy teaching us to wash our faces and where to catch food that she forgot to tell us. And only The Terrific Thief figured it out.

"Humans give us bread and seeds," Flippy says. "But they also yell at us if we sit on their tables."

"And when we poop on them," Mippy says. "Poop is nothing to yell about."

"Humans make no sense," Flippy tells me.

"True, true, true," Mippy says.

"Chester knows how to tell if a human is good or bad," I say. "Please ask him for me."

"Certainly not," Flippy says. "Chester is far scarier than a loud woman in red pants."

"Yes, yes, yes," Mippy says. "Not *yes* that we'll ask him, but *yes* what Flippy said."

"I'll ask him," Kippy says. "He doesn't growl or bark at me. I'm quiet."

And with that, he flies off in the direction of the museum.

"Gracious," I say. "That's unexpected."

We wait for a few hours without saying much. Flippy and Mippy dart around and I nap. The sun starts its slow summer setting over the city.

Kippy does not come back.

"Maybe Chester ate him," Flippy says.

"Chester would never hurt someone who didn't hurt him," I say.

But the three of us know something we don't want to say out loud. The city is a dangerous place for a shy sparrow flying alone.

KIPPY

WE WAIT AND wait but Kippy does not come back.

"Oh, dear," Flippy says.

"Oh, oh, oh," says Mippy.

"He's fine," I say. But my insides are tight with worry. *He's okay,* I tell myself. Over and over until I believe it.

Flippy and Mippy finally leave. It's nice to have friends, but I also like the quiet of no one else on my roof. I avoid Rachel but I eat the food she brings. Another day passes and another. The sparrows do not come back, which means that Kippy is safe. If something had happened to him, Flippy and Mippy would come to tell me. That's what I tell myself as I try not to worry about him.

More sunsets come and I lose track of how many days Rachel feeds me.

And then, finally! The woman in the blue shirt returns!

She looks happy and rested. My whole body makes its engine noise. Not just my throat. Every bit of me is glad she's home.

"Oh, Harvey," she says. "I learned so much!"

She shows me photos of Kraków and of the kitchen where she went every day.

"Were there any cats in Poland?" I ask. "What does Rachel call you? Please, tell me your name."

But she just scratches my ears and life on the roof returns to normal.

At night, her stories are full of how many paczki (POONCH-keys) the bakery sells. How long the line at the bakery is. How a newspaper wrote an article about how she flew to Poland to learn how to cook the paczki.

"Look," she says, when she shows it to me. "This is so good for business!"

There is a photo of her with a tray of paczki in the middle of black squiggles on the soft white paper.

"The bakery is so busy now," she says. "Every morning, we have more and more people in line who want to buy all the things we bake."

She is tired at night, but always says hello to the plants, and we sit while she drinks her tea. We watch the sun set. Even though she is "so busy" at the bakery, time with her is always lazy and happy.

It is quiet and perfect.

But still, whenever the woman in the blue shirt scratches my ears and my throat makes the train noise, I wonder: Why do I let her touch me but run away from Rachel? How can I learn what brave city cats would know? And how will I ever be brave until I know what they do? I am surprised that Kippy never came to tell me what Chester said. Maybe he forgot or just couldn't get close enough to ask. I know he is safe.

I say it over and over to make it true.

ℭ

The summer is in full force and so the sparrows don't visit. When the city is very hot, birds rest near the fountains in the city's parks.

Park fountains have shade and cool water for birds to splash in. There are lots of people nearby who drop lots of crumbs. Fountains are too noisy and wet for cats, but perfect for sparrows.

I myself rest under the tower where there is shade and a breeze. It's where I take all of my naps. One day, in the middle of a nap, I hear, "Ahoy, my young friend."

Those are Chester's words, but certainly not his voice. I look on the ledge. No one. I look near the pots. Nope.

"Ahoy," says the voice again. "Above you."

I look up, and there's Kippy perched on one of the tower's slippery bars.

"Chester's so glad to hear that you have a place," he says. "He says it's what every city creature needs."

I am a little jealous that Kippy saw Chester. "Did he explain about humans?"

"I'm not sure," Kippy says. "But he told me to tell you a story. Do you want to hear it?"

I swish my tail, which is how cats sometimes say yes. Or no.

"Please don't do that," Kippy says. "It makes me nervous."

A swish of the tail is also how a cat might say *I'm going to eat you*. I apologize, and he tells me Chester's story.

ᴗ�

As you know, I had a human once. I was young and he was old and together we both grew older. I trusted him to take me on walks, feed me, and put out soft beds where I could sleep. He trusted me to be glad to see him, to keep him company, and to care how he was. In this way, we were attached.

If they live long enough, all city creatures get old or sick. Even the humans do.

As mine got older, he became sick. He couldn't get out of bed easily and it was hard for him to bend down to pick up my food dish. He had to move to a place with a NO DOGS ALLOWED sign. Before he left, he sent me to live with his son and grandchildren. "You'll like it," he said. "So many young people to walk with you and play."

Instead, the grandchildren pulled my ears and put marbles in my nose. When I growled after the marble went up my nose, somebody kicked me.

That's when I ran away and became a city dog.

Harvey, you won't always know if or why a human is good or bad. But with each one, you will learn. You will get better at knowing more quickly. You already know a lot. You were right to run away from the boy. You were right to let the woman in the blue shirt touch you. I do not know if you should hide from Rachel. But you will learn.

"That's it?" I ask.

"That's a lot," Kippy says.

"I asked a simple question: How does Chester know if a human is good or terrible," I point out. "But you brought me a story, not an answer."

Kippy flies off the perch. He lands on the ground about a foot away from me.

"A city cat caught my mother and ate her," he says. "Most of the time I'm afraid of you. But I am learning when not to be."

"I don't want to learn," I tell him. "I want to know."

Learning is too dangerous. It's why our mother taught us how to live in the city before we left the dumpster. Everything I learned on my own—to avoid boys with sticks, angry cats, and train conductors with newspapers—I learned from danger.

"I understand," Kippy says.

But he doesn't. The only thing he's afraid of is me.

"Go away," I say.

And he does, which makes me immediately sorry. Of the three sparrows, his is the company I like best.

"Wait, come back," I say, but he's gone.

11

DOUBLE NORMAL

THE SKY AND I watch the trees in the park as they go from green to red. The heat fades away, and the air is sharp with the promise of cold. Colder than normal for this part of the year, but at least the sparrows come back.

They're just as chatty as ever. Except for Kippy, who looks more worried than usual. Or maybe he looks mad at me? I hope he's forgiven me for telling him to go away. I'd smile but that shows my teeth, which would *definitely* make him more worried.

"The fountains are empty now," Flippy says.

"Summer is all gone," Mippy says. "Yes, yes, yes."

"Your human is famous," says Flippy. "Because of the bakery."

"She's not my human," I remind them. "I don't live with her. We share the roof."

I don't know what makes humans good or terrible, but at least I still live under the sky. I'm not brave, but I am a city creature.

"Her bakery was in the newspaper," says Mippy.

"I know that, she showed me," I tell them. "Tell me what I don't know."

"What do you mean?" asks Flippy.

"How are the train stations?" I ask. "Have you seen my sister?"

"So many people use the train to buy breakfast at your human's bakery," Flippy says.

"So many," says Mippy.

"She's not my human," I say again, but feel sad this time.

"People at the bakery drop lots of crumbs for us," says Mippy.

This is the problem with sparrows: It is hard to make them focus. I try again.

"What do you know about my sister? Is she okay in her cage? Also, how is the The Terrific Thief?"

I know he is brave and fierce, but when you chase food and safety all day, it's always possible that hunger and danger will win. Even my brave brother could wind up *SPLAT*.

Mippy starts to speak but Kippy holds up his wing and says, "Tell him the bad news."

Bad news?! "Is my brother okay? And my sister?"

"She sits in the window," says Flippy. "She looks fine."

"Fine, fine, fine," Mippy says.

"And The Terrific Thief?" I ask.

"He lives near a building on the University campus."

"And he eats from the University dumpster," Mippy says. "He does, he does, he does."

"We have to tell him about the park," Kippy says.

He says it quietly but firmly. His feathers ruffle, which tells me he's also frustrated by how the sparrows can't focus.

"The squirrels in the park are eating double," Flippy says.

"They say lots of cold and ice and snow is coming," Mippy adds.

"Double the normal amount," Kippy says. "It's serious."

I've only been alive for six winters. But I've heard the stories from older city creatures. Stories about how a terrible and fierce winter can arrive and refuse to leave. How that kind of winter makes it hard to chase after food and safety—and easy for hunger and danger to catch us.

During a hard winter a lot of us die from the cold. This is why it's so important to have your own spot—a safe, warm place where a hard winter can't find you.

"High above the city is colder than on the street," Kippy says. "The wind is stronger and the air sharper."

"The roof was safe last winter," Flippy says. "This winter, danger might catch you."

"Because of the cold," Mippy says. "True, true, true."

"You have to leave the roof," says Flippy.

"Go down into the city?" I ask.

I don't want to do that. The roof is the only safe place I know.

"No," Kippy says. "You can't go into the city."

"It's more dangerous there than here," Flippy says. "More dangerous than ever."

"Everyone is fighting for a good place," Mippy says.

"They know a hard winter is coming," Flippy explains. "Everyone knows they will need a safe, warm place."

"So many fights," says Mippy. "So many!"

"We think you should live with the woman in the blue shirt," Kippy murmurs softly.

"I can't," I say.

"Why?" Kippy asks.

My list. Everything important to me would be permanently impossible. I can't save my brother or repay Chester for his kindness if I live inside with a human. It's true I'd always have food and safety. And I'd probably learn her name. But I'd never be brave like a fierce city cat.

"Why can't you?" Flippy asks.

"Why, why—" Mippy starts to say. But Kippy and Flippy say HUSH and so she does.

They're sparrows. They won't understand about lists or being brave. After all, they aren't supposed to be brave. When they run away, it's called flying.

I just say what's true: "I can't."

Kippy's feathers ruffle again, and this time, it's because he's frustrated with me. But all three accept my answer and fly off.

And then, one cold morning, the woman in the blue shirt doesn't come.

12

TRAIN WRECK

I REMEMBER THAT she's busy with the long lines at the bakery and how sometimes she puts my food down with a *clink* and says, "Harvey, I must dash. I'm late."

Perhaps today, she is too busy even for that. "She will come tomorrow," I say to the orange pots. They don't answer.

But she doesn't come the next day. My stomach makes a grumbling, fumbling, angry sound. It's a sound my stomach made a lot when I lived down in the city.

It means that I'm hungry. It's not a nice sound. It reminds me of what a train would sound like if it crashed.

I look at my water dish. It is half empty and I drink half of it. I'm still hungry. I haven't been hungry since I ran up to the roof. Another tomorrow comes, but she doesn't.

I drink the rest of my water. I try to remember what I did when I was hungry before I ran up the stairs. I looked for food in garbage cans, under café tables, behind restaurants, and in train stations.

None of those things are on the roof. There's only the tower and a circle of pots with dried up winter plants. *Thump thump whoosh.* It's a strange sound. I haven't heard it in a long time. *Thump thump whoosh.* I don't like it. But I know what it means. I'm not only hungry, I'm afraid.

A cat can only be hungry for so long before it dies.

I have to leave the roof. And to do that, I'll have to go down the stairs. All those stairs I ran up so long ago. The ones I didn't count. *It's time, Harvey*, I think.

There's a swish in the air and then two more right after it.

"Where is the woman in the blue shirt?" I ask them.

The three of them squawk, flutter, and mutter to each other.

"We don't know," Flippy and Mippy say together.

They hate not to know.

"I'm hungry," I say.

I hope they will help me think of a way to find food here on the roof. Instead they all—not just Kippy—look alarmed and fly back a little bit.

"I'm not going to eat *you*," I say, but they stay back.

Their small black eyes are large with fear.

"I'm the one who should be afraid," I tell them. "I have to go down all the stairs. Do boys live in this building?"

"Lots of them," says Flippy.

"Yes, yes, yes," Mippy says. "Lots and lots of them."

"All you have to do is go to the alley behind the building," Kippy says softly. "There are garbage cans there."

That might be the nicest thing anyone has ever said to me.

"Can you see if there are any boys on the stairs?" I ask.

The sparrows fly over to the door of the stairs. They flit around it.

"No one's there . . . right now," Flippy says. "But there might be someone we can't see or hear."

"True, true, true," Mippy says.

Fear and hunger fight inside my body. My stomach makes its grumbling, fumbling, angry sound. My heart goes *thump thump whoosh*. I can't think.

Harvey, you can do this. There's a shiver under my fur. *I can't.* Behind me, the sparrows swish around.

I walk down one step. And then two. And three.

Before I know it, I'm on a landing where there are two doors and a potted plant. No boys. I sniff the plant and then sneeze right away. The dirt is not the good-smelling kind like on the roof. I go down one more flight. It also has two doors, but no plants. It smells like onion, cabbage, and meat. My nose fills with hungry smells. One of the doors opens and it's a boy! We look at each other.

"Ma!" the boy says, looking behind him. He says it very loudly. "Ma, come here! Ma!"

He sounds like a pigeon. Pigeons are only annoying, not dangerous. I'm not afraid and scoot down the stairs in a blur of fur and whiskers. Before I know it, I'm on the next landing.

Two doors, no plants, and no smells.

I walk down another flight to a landing that has a big, pretty plant between the doors. It smells a lot like the ones on the roof.

"Hello," I say.

It doesn't answer me. Plants are useless. I scratch and meow at both doors just in case they belong to the woman in the blue shirt. But no one comes.

I look down. I see stairs, one last landing, more stairs, and then a front door out into the city. The city with its garbage cans, restaurants, and alleys. With its humans who yell, cranky dogs, and shiny cars. *Bad things might happen*, I tell myself, *but also good ones.*

I go down the next set of stairs as easy as you please.

While I sniff the potted plant on the landing (it's a heavy, yucky smell), one of the doors opens. I look up, ready to hiss if it's another boy. But it's Rachel in the bright red pants.

"Why, Harvey," she says. "How marvelous!"

I'm hungry and you're loud. What's marvelous about that?

And then she scoops me up! With such cold hands! NO ONE HAS EVER PICKED ME UP. I'm so surprised that I hiss and scratch at her!

"*Ooohhhwww!*" Rachel says in her loud way.

Thunk, I'm on the ground. And like a shot, I'm down the stairs.

"Wait, Harvey, wait," I hear her call.

But I don't. And in a flash, I am below.

Down here, the sun is too far away. And the noise is too close by.

I'd forgotten how the city folds itself into you. I wish I'd asked Kippy the fastest way to the alley, but smells are things to listen for using your nose. And garbage is a loud smell.

I follow it left, left, and left. As I walk down the alley to its three black garbage bins, I look forward to making my way through their disgusting mess. That's how hungry I am.

I take a deep sniff: bits of fatty dinner scraps, tins that aren't quite empty, and a pizza box with cheese and greasy meat. And underneath it all, the prize of all prizes: bacon. The city can be a marvelous host and I send out my thanks to the gods of garbage.

But then, I hear a low growl. It's attached to yellow eyes and bald patches on angry orange fur.

A true city cat—fierce and terrifying.

13

MR. BOOTS

"HOW DO YOU do?" I say.

"Beat it, Stripy," she says.

I think about the rat in the hospital dumpster. "I'll thank you to call me Mr. Boots."

"You do have some nice white fur there," she says. "But this is my place. Go away."

Go away, shoo, shoo. I used to hear that every day. I don't like it.

"I realize this is your place," I say. "But even you can't eat everything here. Might I have what you don't finish?"

I can't imagine The Terrific Thief or even my mother, polite as she was, ever asking permission, but at least I'm not running away. And this cat is bigger than the rat was.

"You can take the bin on the end," the city cat says. "But nothing else."

Hurrah! It's a fairly generous offer. No bacon, of course, but bits of lamb chops and part of a roast chicken that's almost spoiled but not quite. I pull chicken from the soggy carcass. And then I find a container with beef soup stuck along the sides. I lick it up and up and up.

"You've had enough, Boots," says the alley's owner, much too soon.

"It's Mr. Boots, if you please," I say with as much dignity as I can over a mouthful of scraps.

Being called *Mr. Boots* by a fierce city cat reminds me of my mother and I like that.

This cat looks at me with her large yellow eyes. "Life is hard, Mr. Boots."

I wonder if life is harder for her than it is for me. After all, I know Chester and the sparrows. I have the roof. At least, I had the roof. I had the woman in the blue shirt. What could have happened to her and will the roof ever be a safe place again?

"Do you have a warm place?" I ask. "I hear it's going to be such a cold winter."

"I sleep behind these bins and I eat from them," she says. "I'm not afraid of winter."

Of course she isn't. She's one of those perfectly brave cats.

"What's your name?" I ask.

"Everyone calls me Captain."

"Captain?" I say, turning it over in my mouth like a food I've never eaten.

"I was born on a ferry boat," she says. "I lived there a long time until I lost my place in a fight."

"I'm so sorry," I say. "I know that's hard."

"It's the only fight I've ever lost, and it was to a much bigger cat," Captain says, sounding proud. "But I chased two cats and a small dog out of here, and now it's mine."

I feel sad and worried for those cats and the small dog who probably shared these bins quite happily before Captain showed up.

"Do you ever get tired?" I ask, thinking of all the fighting it takes to live.

"You ask a lot of questions," she says.

"You seem very wise," I say, which is true. "And I need to know a lot of things."

"You're a funny one, Mr. Boots," she says. "Do I ever get tired of what?"

"Chasing food and rushing away from danger," I say. "Life."

It's no wonder I napped so often on the roof. I've spent my whole life in the city running.

"If we didn't do it, we'd be hungry," Captain points out. "Or *SPLAT.*"

"Is having food and safety enough?" After all, my list has more on it than catching those two things.

"I have the sky," she says. "I have everything I need."

It's what you'd expect from a brave city cat, but she must be cold sometimes. The alley isn't cozy like Chester's drainpipe. But maybe Captain knows what Chester didn't.

"What about humans?" I ask. "How do you know if they are good or terrible?"

"That's easy," she says. "All of them are terrible."

"None of them have ever given you food?" I ask. "Even on the ferry?"

"Of course not," she says. "I catch everything I eat."

Even though Mrs. Gianni usually yelled at me, when she did give me food, it was often the only meal I'd have. And the mayor's granddaughter once gave me a bowl of milk. It made up for how loud she was. Plus, people in cafés would drop things on purpose for me or the sparrows.

I can't imagine life in the city without food from humans. Even though I don't know how to tell the good ones from the terrible.

"Humans are dangerous," Captain says. "Now, go away."

I take one more bite of soggy chicken and she pins her ears back and shows her teeth.

"Beat it."

My scar from the last cat fight still itches. So, I beat it back to the sidewalk with a half-full belly and a sad heart. Captain is exactly the kind of brave city cat I want to be: a fierce fighter with a safe place and no fears about the hard winter.

I have everything I need, she said. But even though she has food and shelter, the alley isn't quiet and perfect. There's no one to tell Captain that what she does is splendid.

I miss the woman in the blue shirt and I'm worried. In the city, danger catches humans, too.

14

FLY AWAY HOME

BUT I HAVE to consider the possibility that she got tired of visiting me.

Humans are famous for living with animals and then giving them away. Sometimes, humans even leave animals out on the street or at the jail they call a shelter. When that happens, the creatures who used to live *with* a human wind up all alone in jail, scared and confused, for no reason. It's horrible but true. Humans are confusing and often awful.

But the woman in the blue shirt never said *Beat it* or *Go away, shoo shoo*. I want to find her. She's the best part of the city.

If she's not on the roof or in the building under the roof, then where to look?

The bakery, of course! Of course, the bakery!

The bakery that's so far away. *So far.*

I make a small map in my head of how to get there. The street with the good garbage cans and the bakery is thirty streets away from the library, which is twenty streets away from the park. I can see the park from the roof, so all I have to do is find the park, get across it, and then walk fifty streets.

My heart sinks into my paws for a moment. Crossing fifty streets is a lot of walking near cars that can hit you and make you go *SPLAT*. I'm out of practice avoiding so many cars, at avoiding so much danger. I wish cars didn't go so fast.

Harvey, you can do this, I tell myself. *Better start, you've a long way to go.*

Of course, I've no idea which way the park is. From the roof, I can see it *and* the entire city. On the street, I only see a bit at a time. I pick a direction and hope for the best.

I cross the first street. It's easy—no cars whiz by. The next few ones are also easy. The fifth street has lots of humans waiting to cross it and many cars racing down it. I stand between the curb and a streetlight so that none of the humans can step on, yell at, or kick me.

When the humans start to cross, I slip into the crowd they make. I get to the other side. My whole body loosens in relief. I keep walking. I walk and walk, always slipping and hiding. But I don't find the park.

I must be going the wrong way. I'll have to go back to the building under my roof and try another direction. The thought of walking all that way makes me as heavy and cold as wet fur.

I turn to face all those streets again and remind myself that I want to find the woman in the blue shirt. That I want to know if danger caught her or if she's done with me in that way humans get with animals. I conjure up my roof, her plants, and the way we like to sit.

She's not that kind of human.

I cross two very busy streets and then rest at a quiet one. I'm so tired and hungry. I start to cross it, and—

Out of nowhere, a bicycle *WHIZZES* down the street. I freeze and stare. Fear means I can't move. The bicycle swerves and the human on it yells, *Stupid cat!* The human who yells has on red pants.

No one likes getting yelled at, but the pants remind me of Rachel. I'm afraid of her but also so tired that the bike almost made me *SPLAT*. My mother was hit by a bus when she was tired. If I find Rachel, I'll find the woman in the blue shirt and I won't have to walk all the way to the bakery. The risk of *SPLAT*, I decide, is more dangerous than Rachel. *Harvey, you can do this.*

The whole way back to the building under my roof, I'm careful crossing and watching. *So careful.* When I finally get there, I go slowly up two flights of stairs to the door that smells like cinnamon and oranges.

I scratch and meow until Rachel opens the door.

"Oh, thank goodness," she says. "I was so worried."

"I was so hungry," I tell her. "I'm sorry I scratched you. Please tell me where to find the woman in the blue shirt."

All she hears, of course, is *meowrrr meowwwr.* She reaches down with her cold hands onto my fur and I'm flying up into the air.

"Let's go," she says.

She says it loudly, but I stay very still and do not hiss or scratch. Rachel walks briskly up the stairs. She stops at the landing with the pots that smelled like the ones on the roof. She takes a key from her pocket and opens one of the apartment doors.

Rachel puts me down and closes the door. I jump over a large sofa and up onto a shelf by a window. It's higher up than the sidewalk, but from it, I can only see

across the street, not the whole city. And I can only see a small part of the sky.

"I found Harvey," Rachel calls out. "He came back."

Rachel goes into another room. I hear voices. One of them is soft and gentle. I know that voice! I follow it into a room with a big bed in the middle. There are windows and a blue chair on one side. On the other side are shelves and drawers. There are piles of clothes and books all over the floor.

I hop onto the bed. There she is—the same as always but different. Now her leg is in a big white cage.

PART THREE

IN HERE

15

A DIFFERENT SKY

"HARVEY, I'M SO sorry no one has fed you," she says. "I broke my leg and when I went to the hospital, I forgot to call Rachel."

I want to tell her it's okay, but instead I nudge her hand. She scratches my ears until the *hhhhmmm* sound comes out. And also, my hungry sound.

"Rachel, will you bring him a dish from the kitchen?" she asks.

"Danielle, you can't let him eat on the bed," Rachel says.

Danielle? That's a good name for someone who is quiet and smells like mint. And I finally know it! One item off my list.

"Yes, I can," Danielle says.

I want to stick my tongue out at Rachel, but I don't. Here's what I do instead: Eat an entire dish of cheese and chicken. Eat another one. I am grateful when Rachel puts a box of dirt and sand in a small tiled room. Now my bathroom is in Danielle's bathroom. After eating a lot of food on a mostly empty stomach, a bathroom is important.

After Rachel leaves, it is quiet. I curl up on the bed. Danielle scratches my ears again.

"I know you don't like to be inside," she says. "But I hope you'll stay."

Stay? Live here? What's wrong with the roof? I look at her and tilt my head. She seems to understand that as a question.

"If I don't see you every day, I worry about you," she says. "And I can't get up to the roof with my leg. Will you live here?"

I've only ever lived under the sky. I think about Captain behind her garbage bins. Chester under his drainpipe. My brother on the University campus. If I stay here, I'll never be a real city cat.

"It would be such a relief if you did," she says. "I've missed you."

I have missed her, too. Missed her so much.

"I'll think about it," I tell her.

I find the warmest, softest spot, right next to her. A box by the window clanks and hisses. Danielle turns the pages of her book. These are strange noises yet nice ones. I am full and warm. And then I am asleep.

I wake up in dark, heavy air. From the window, you can hardly see any of the sky's silver lights. Danielle is asleep. Her leg in its white cage looks like a park bench that just got painted.

I hop off the bed and go to the noisy box by the window. It's warm. From here, the city's lights are yellow and brighter than the sky's silver ones.

I look up at the ceiling. Above it is not the sky, but a landing with a boy and his "Ma." I look down at the floor. It's not a roof or a sidewalk or a courtyard. Below it is Rachel. I jump off the box and onto the chair by the bed.

I look at Danielle and curl up on the chair. I guess I'll stay a while.

ꝏ

If time slowed down on the roof, it speeds up inside. Not because I have to find food and run from danger (I do not do that here), but because everything here is the opposite of life outside. The air is warm even though I can see how white and cold the city is.

On the roof, the city's noises were far away. But here, when I press my nose against the glass and look down at the street below, I *see* the cars and people go by, but never *hear* them.

Strangest of all is that it's impossible to know exactly when the sun comes up or when it sets. Days pass, but the beginnings and endings happen without my seeing them.

If I took a lot of naps on the roof, I am too busy now. There is so much to do.

Sometimes, Danielle holds a stuffed mouse by the tail, and I pretend to chase it. When I crawl under her bed blankets, I'm a BRAVE CITY CAT stalking the streets. Or I'm an OWL swooping through the park.

Of course, I'm really only ever Harvey. And all I find under the covers is Danielle or one of her books. Once I found a piece of toast that she dropped, but I left it there. Cats do not like toast.

But guess what we do like? Wet food!

It's not disgusting at all. It's chopped fish or chicken or duck that magically comes from a can. There's a thing called a can opener. The noise it makes is my new favorite noise. *Click, clunk, click, clunk.* And, presto, the can is open.

I eat out of a dish that Danielle says she once used for cereal. Now it's mine. Sometimes I eat with her in the kitchen. And sometimes we eat on the bed. The bed and the food are excellent parts of a life with no sky.

Sometimes Danielle and I are quiet and perfect, but lots of times we are a noisy mess. Especially when I help with the dishes. I stand next to the sink and try to catch the water from the faucet. I can never catch it, and the water goes everywhere.

The sparrows would love it. It's sad that they will never live with a human.

But now I'm happy that my sister does. She has wet food and the funny upside-down world of inside, just like me.

I cross off *Save sister from brick cage* from my collection of impossible things. I have food and safety, just as I did on the roof. I know Danielle's name. All that's left is to repay Chester and be brave like a true city cat. At some point, I will have to figure out how to accomplish those ever-more-impossible items.

But for now, Danielle and I eat, sleep, and have fun.

Her leg gets better bit by bit. The big white cage becomes a small black one. It's called a walking cast. She starts to go to the bakery every day. When she comes home, we sit on the couch while she has tea. We eat, do dishes, and then talk or play until bedtime.

When she's at the bakery, I discover so many things to do: I jump up on all the counters in the kitchen. I sit on the stove. I nap in the bathtub. I climb the tall shelves and knock books down. Or I stand on the very top shelf and put my paw right against the ceiling.

"I can touch the sky," I announce to the empty apartment.

I know the ceiling is not the same as the sky all *true* city cats live under. But here, it's not the sky that says, *All is well, have no fear.* Here, the sky doesn't say, *You can do it, go find food.* In here, Danielle says all the things the sky did out there. In here, Danielle is the sky.

And, just like the real sky, Danielle can bring bad weather. Only Danielle's bad weather isn't rain or snow.

Danielle's bad weather is worse. It's Rachel.

16

FRIENDS

WHEN SHE COMES, I jump right under the bed. There are huge piles of dust there. Also, one slipper, two books, and some boxes. All of them are fun to play with.

Rachel is not.

But she comes to visit three or four nights a week. Danielle cooks dinner. They eat. They talk and laugh. Danielle says Rachel is her friend. It doesn't matter. I still run under the bed when Rachel comes.

"I guess he doesn't like you," Danielle says after a month or two.

"That makes sense," Rachel says. "I don't like cats."

Who doesn't like cats? That is the dumbest thing I've ever heard. I'm sure Danielle is going to yell at her for being so dumb. But she doesn't.

"I know you're a dog person," she says. "I just hope Harvey's not afraid of you."

"Harvey's never afraid," Rachel says. "That cat climbed the water tower. All of the city's pigeons are terrified of him. Plus, he came looking for you. Harvey's the bravest soul we know."

I remember the time on the roof when Rachel looked for me *under* the pots. I remember how I thought she was not very smart. And yet right now I think she is the most amazing and brilliant creature in the world. Humans are confusing. They're so many things at once.

Why can't they understand our words? I want to tell Rachel, *Thank you so much for calling me brave.*

I leave the dusty boxes, the slipper, and the books. I stand in the bedroom doorway. I remind myself that this is *my* apartment. Not Rachel's. My bed and my food dish are here. Even my bathroom.

I have no reason to be afraid. Danielle sees me and clucks softly. *Kuh, tuk, kuk.*

Rachel sits on the couch, which is also mine. I walk over to her. Her red pants are very bright. The way she smells makes my nose itch.

But I am the bravest soul she knows.

I nudge my head against her leg. I wait for her hand to touch my ears. Nothing. I remember that sometimes she is not very smart. So I nudge again. Her fingers come down to rub along my back and then down my tail.

Normally, I don't like to have my tail touched, but I forgive her. Then she pulls on the tips of my ears and folds them.

What's wrong with her?

"Don't fold them," Danielle says. "Cats only like to be touched behind their ears."

I feel Rachel's fingers rub all around my ears in a gentle way. It is surprisingly nice.

"You should get a cat," Danielle says.

"I want a dog," Rachel says. "But I haven't met the right one. The last dog I loved was a calm, good soul."

I think of how Chester used to have a human but now sleeps under a drainpipe. I think of his calm soul. Of how good he is. I might not want to live with Rachel, but I'm not a dog. And she probably has a bed. And a can opener.

She lifts her hand away from me and goes back to her dinner. I walk to the window and press against the glass. I can't feel the air so I don't know how soon winter will end. But it always does.

And then we'll go up to the roof.

I will ask Kippy to tell Chester to come here.

And then Rachel can meet the right dog.

ℒ

Only it's much harder to get out of the apartment than it was to get in it. At first, Danielle goes to the roof without me!

"Harvey, I just don't want anything to happen to you," she says.

Happen to me? I own that roof. It's mine. But she keeps me from following her.

"No, no, no," she says. "You stay here."

I sit at the front door and scratch at it, over and over and over, until one afternoon she scoops me up.

"Okay, Harvey, I get it," she says. "But no running off or you will break my heart."

I happen to know you can't break a heart. It's not like a leg. I press my head into her chest where her heart is. *No running off*, I say. *I promise.*

Then she does the worst thing—she carries me up the stairs! As if I don't know how to run up those stairs! So embarrassing! Thankfully, she puts me down right before we get out to the roof.

What if anyone had seen that?

OLD TIMES

YET ONCE I'M outside, I forget everything but the way soft blue air pours down on me like water on dry sand.

"Hello sky," I say.

I smell the plants. The earth is still dark, the pots are still orange, and the bushes are still fat. There are no flowers yet, but there will be.

I stand under the tower and look up. Compared to the ceiling at Danielle's, the tower is small. So small! I remember all the times it kept me dry, gave me shade, or helped me to hide from Rachel.

"Hello tower," I say.

Danielle digs in her pots. I curl up in the sun and watch. And wait until there's a swish in the air. And then two more.

"Hello, Harvey," Flippy says. "We thought we'd never see you again."

"Never, never, never," Mippy says.

I ask Kippy, "Will you give Chester a message from me?"

"No, no, no," Mippy says.

"We don't know where he is," Flippy explains.

"Under the drainpipe behind the museum," I say.

"He isn't," Kippy says.

"Of course he is," I say. "It's his place."

"It *was* his place," says Flippy.

"There was a fight for it last winter," Mippy says.

"It belongs to another dog now, Harvey," Kippy says. "I'm sorry we have to tell you that."

"A bigger dog," Mippy says. "A younger one."

"One with more teeth," Flippy says.

"Is Chester hurt?" I ask.

The sparrows don't say anything.

"Tell me!"

"I think he was," Kippy says. "But he ran off into the park before we could find out."

My heart is beating into my ears. But it's not a *thump thump whoosh* sound. It's a command: *Find. Him. Now.*

I look at Danielle. Cats do not break promises.

But I need to find Chester.

"Such a lovely day," she says, looking back at me. "Just like old times."

Danielle makes sure I always have food and safety. She showed me why my sister doesn't need saving. I know her name.

Danielle *is* my list.

What if I never see her again? A bus could roll over me. Hunger could chase me until I am lost. I imagine life without Danielle, and my whole inside twists and turns in a way that feels like a rip.

So that is how a heart breaks, I think.

And yet.

I must find Chester. It's one thing to fail at being brave. That's only embarrassing. But to fail a creature who helped you when you had nothing? That's unacceptable. And Chester is . . . Chester is worth a thousand broken hearts. He's worth mine. And now is the time to repay all his kindness.

"I'll be back," I tell Danielle. "I promise."

And then I run. I run right down the stairs, past all the landings, and out the door. I run until I am on the sidewalk and back into the city.

I look up at the sky, now far away. The last time I was on this sidewalk, I was hungry beyond hungry. I hear footsteps and know Danielle is running down the stairs after me. I'm lucky humans are so slow.

Which way is the park?! Last time, did I go left or right? *Think, Harvey, think.*

"Harvey, I can help!" I look up and there's Kippy. He's perched on the lowest branch of a scraggly sidewalk tree.

"Go straight and then left at the corner! I'll be your lookout."

A WALK IN THE PARK

WHEN NO ONE is chasing you, running down the street is the best part of being a city cat. You're suddenly part of the smells and the sounds. All the busy, tired, happy, and sad feelings in the air belong to you.

Turns out that the park is only three quiet streets away from where Danielle lives. There are no cars and no humans as I run. I run until I am the city. I run until the city is me. I run until we are the same.

In other words, I run into the park.

"You made it!" Kippy hovers two feet above me. "Now use your nose and find Chester."

"It doesn't work like that," I say.

"But you're a cat—you can smell anything."

I sigh and remind myself that even a smart bird has a bird-sized brain. Even so, Kippy must know you have to listen for smells. If we wanted to find yesterday's milk, it would be as obvious as fifty people shouting. But we are after the smell of an older dog who has lost his safe place, which sounds more like the last breeze before sunset. Not obvious at all.

Plus, the park is smack in the middle of the city. It smells like everything: grass and trees, playgrounds, buses, lunch, poop, birds, and mustard.

If I try to find Chester by smell, Kippy and I will be here for three months.

We have to narrow the area down. I think of two things Chester always said: that if you don't have your own place, a good spot is under a park bench. And that when you're scared, you run as far as possible from the spot that scared you.

I certainly know that's true from A LOT of experience.

The drainpipe behind the museum is by the park's east entrance. We are at the park's west entrance.

"Let's go to the benches by the north entrance," I say. "It's the farthest away from the east entrance."

"The south entrance is farther away than the north one is," Kippy says.

"No, it isn't."

"It is," he insists.

Cats do not argue with birds. I simply say, "Follow me."

I sniff my way under each of the five benches near the north entrance. They stink of cigarettes and flat soda. Chester smells like warm bread and wet dirt. There's no trace of him.

"Maybe you were right," I say. "Let's try the south entrance."

I keep my eye on Kippy as we walk. He'll see Chester first because he's higher up and ahead of me.

If Chester's not in the park, we will have to look in all of the city's food places. It will take a long time to search the whole city, and it'll be dark by the time I get home.

Danielle thinks I ran off. And no matter what I do, I won't be able to explain. All she'll hear is gibberish.

I stop walking because of an awful thought: Danielle might not let me back in to live with her. I wouldn't want to live with a cat who broke a promise. Would you?

"HEY, MOVE THAT STUPID CAT!"

I look around. And then I panic. I'm in the middle of a playing field. A playing field full of boys! Two groups of boys are in the middle of that terrifying game where they hit a ball with a stick and then run. One group of boys stands in the field and the other lines up behind a boy with the stick.

The stick is not sharp or long, but it's very thick. I've heard about humans who use it to hit dogs. It's one of the scariest weapons I've seen.

The boy who yelled holds the stick over his shoulder. My lungs get tight and my paws feel heavy. I try to move but can't. It's like when the bicycle was coming at me. Kippy swishes and swooshes above me.

"Run," he says.

I want to, of course, but fear is fear.

"I can't," I tell him.

"Maybe he's lost," a boy in the middle of the field and close to me says.

This boy holds the ball in his hand. His other hand is trapped in a big leather envelope. I notice that he's speaking softly.

"Nobody move," he says.

And although he is talking to all the boys on the field, he keeps his voice low. And in that moment, I know two things:

1. Chester was right after all: I've
   learned to tell if a human is good.

---

2. This is a good human.

This boy is quiet. He doesn't come to me. He's waiting for me to show him it's okay. Just like Danielle used to do when she'd put the food down and say, *Kuh, tuk, kuk.* I take a step toward him.

"Come on, let's play!" the boy with the stick yells.

Some of the other boys yell at him to *SHUT UP.*

I ignore everything. Including the boy with the big stick. I take another step.

"Hey, there, buddy," the boy with the ball says. "You on your way somewhere?"

I nod. I am on my way somewhere.

"We're all going to sit down so that we don't spook you." He sits down. "See?"

"Yeah, cool," says another boy, and sits. All of the boys in the field sit.

"I'm not sitting down," says the boy with the stick.

"Because you're a jerk," says the boy with the ball. To me, he says, "Go on, buddy."

There's something about him—a calm kindness—that makes me think of Chester. I go right to him and press my head against his knee. *Thank you,* I say. And then I march out of the field while Kippy flits around and around.

Behind us, I hear the boys' voices.

"So weird!" one of them says.

"Cool," says another one. Also, "Next batter, you're up!"

They've totally forgotten about me. We're free.

Once we are far from the field, Kippy says, "You're not afraid of boys anymore."

"I'm afraid," I say, still able to feel how I froze in place, unable to move. "Just not as much as I was."

"But you touched one," he says. "How can you do that if you're afraid?"

"You can be scared and still do things," I remind him. "You're scared of cats and spend time with me."

"Well," he says. "I can fly higher than you can jump."

"Well," I say. "You notice I did not touch the boy with the stick."

"I did notice that," Kippy says.

We laugh and keep moving. I walk, and he flies. My body is used to walking from the bed to the couch. Or from the chair back to the bed. All this outdoor walking is like climbing to the top of the bookcase fifty times.

"Can you see how much farther we have to go?"

"About the distance of ten streets?" Kippy says. "I'm not sure."

The sun is beginning to slip down. It will be dark soon. *Chester, please let us find you.*

We pass trees, people, a fountain, more people, more trees, and then the park's small café. I spent two hours under the tables there once, looking for food. I got yelled at instead.

That's the city for you.

Up ahead is the last group of trees before the south entrance. They make up a little grove that never has food but almost always has rats. Kippy disappears into it and then comes flying straight back. He lands right in front of me.

"I found Chester! I think he's being held prisoner!"

Birds can be very dramatic. I wait.

"There are all these dogs jumping on his head!"

"That doesn't sound like prison," I tell him, but it doesn't sound great.

We come to the edge of the grove. I hear barking, but it's not Chester's bark. I sniff the tallest of the trees. Do I remember how to do this?

My nails grab the tree's bark and my muscles push. And, presto, I'm high up on a thick branch with lots of leaves to hide behind. Kippy lands delicately on a thin branch well above mine.

I look down and there's my Chester. He has a little gray in his muzzle now, but nothing else is different. We've found him.

Only he's covered in floppy ears and huge paws. The barking is from four squiggly puppies.

SOMETHING TO LOSE

HOW CAN SMALL dogs make so much noise? Chester's quiet and calm, the way I remember. His silence is louder than all the puppy noise. They bark and jump on his head. He doesn't look happy, but he certainly doesn't look like a prisoner.

The puppies have glossy black fur with brown spots on their faces and paws. One of them has white spots mixed in with the brown.

"Chester!"

He looks up. And then growls and nips the shoulder of the puppy closest to him. All of them fall silent and sit at attention.

"Harvey, hello," he says, as if I appear in a tree every day. "Kippy, good to see you."

The dogs all rush to the foot of the tree and howl.

"This is why I like being high up," Kippy tells me.

"Silence," Chester says. The puppies are quiet, but still stare at me like I am dinner.

"Can we talk privately?" I ask.

"I can't come up," he says. "And I'm guessing you won't come down."

The puppies immediately lie down.

"I'd rather not," I say, although their response to what they thought was a command is impressive. "There's four of them and only one of me."

"They won't move," Chester says. "I promise. Come down and we'll talk."

I trust Chester more than I'm afraid of the puppies. I start down the tree, shut my eyes, and jump. I land with a soft thud, little clouds of dust kicking up under my paws.

The puppies lie between me and Chester. I give them a stern look and stride right past them. After being close to the boys in the park, being near puppies seems easy. Chester sniffs my head.

"You smell like food and safety," he says. "I knew you'd find a place and make it your own. Didn't I always say you would?"

"Well, my place is indoors," I say. "And I didn't fight for it, exactly."

I love my place. It is the best place in the city, only I didn't chase anyone out of it the way my mother did to get our dumpster. But I did get what she never had.

"I have a human now!"

And then I tell him everything. I tell Chester about Danielle's bed, and the ceiling, and the good things to eat. I tell him what Danielle smells like and how she drinks tea and leaves books all over the floor. Stories spill out of me the way water does from a bowl that's too full.

Above me, Kippy coughs, reminding me why we're in the park, far away from my human.

"She's why I'm here!" I tell him. "I have a human for you! She's called Rachel and lives in a safe place!"

I'm so excited that I'm shouting. Finally, I can repay him.

"With food and a bed. Danger and hunger will never find you there," I say. "And she wants a dog. She said so."

"Oh Harvey," Chester says. "I can't leave them."

He points his muzzle to the four puppies, three of whom are trying so hard to be still, they're wiggling.

The one with the white-and-brown spots is the only one who looks as if she has no interest in chasing me.

"They aren't ready to live alone," he says.

"Why are you taking care of them?" I ask. "Where's their mother?"

"Dead," Chester says, in his quiet and calm way. "Hit by a bus, just like yours was."

"Oh," I say, which is not the right thing to say so I add, "I'm sorry. That's hard."

"I found them in the park with no idea about how to do anything."

We were so lucky that our mother died after she'd told us everything we needed to know.

"And you've taught them?" I ask.

"I'm trying to," he says. "They need to learn a lot in order to live in the city."

"But you lost your place behind the museum," I say. "And Rachel has a can opener."

"I remember those," he says, and his eyes cloud up with memory before looking around the grove with pride. "As you can see, I found a new place and now that I've chased out the rats, it's better than the drainpipe."

The minute I jumped down into the little grove, I did feel a cozy safeness. The trees are close enough together to keep out rain and hot sun. The breeze and the light curl gently around the trunks. The ground is soft. But beyond the grove is the city with all its danger.

"The sparrows said the dog who took your place hurt you," I say. "That will never happen if you live with Rachel."

And then I remember how when Chester's human got old, he sent him to live with other humans who hurt him.

"What I mean is, she's young and won't get old for a long time," I say. "She's safe."

"You don't live with your human in order to be safe," Chester says. "You live with her because you're brave."

I snort, which feels like a sneeze that got mixed up with a cough. Cats should not snort. It sounds silly and annoying.

"Don't make fun of me because I'm not brave," I say. "I can't help that I'm not that sort of cat."

"You're the sort of cat who gets attached," Chester says. "To your roof, your annoying sparrows, and now to Danielle."

I swish my tail, which is how cats sometimes say *What is your point?*

"Only the bravest of souls get attached," he says.

"That's not true," I say. "Fighting is what makes a city creature brave."

I think of Captain who lost her fight on the ferry, but then won her next one for sole ownership of the alley. I think of my mother, keeping three kittens safe under a dumpster. I think of The Terrible Thief, risking his life for a feast.

I lived with Danielle after she invited me to. Saying yes was not brave, was it?

But then I think: It has to have been a little brave, or I would have said yes right away. She asked me many times before I agreed to do it. I was afraid to even let her touch me!

"Harvey, I'm not brave because of fights with other dogs."

I start to disagree, and then I think of all the times he lectured a dog for chasing squirrels. All the times he told other creatures to share their places. I think of curling up between his paws, happily safe from the rain.

It's not the fighting that makes Chester fierce and strong.

"I'm brave because I'm attached to what I love," he says. "The drainpipe, you, and now these silly creatures."

I tilt my head and look at him, feeling exactly the way I did when I first lived with Danielle. Everything in my life is now the opposite of what I hoped it would be. But I somehow found a way to do the most impossible item in the collection: Danielle and the roof made me brave. In fact, I scared away pigeons, touched a human, and asked Rachel for help—all because I got attached.

Two of the puppies thump their tails. All of them stare at Chester like he is the sky.

"They're lucky," I say. "But you deserve to be lucky."

"Lucky just means that you love something," Chester says.

"I miss you," I say. "That's why I want you to live with Rachel."

"That's how it goes," Chester says. "When you're brave enough to be attached, you're going to miss something."

I touch my nose to his and feel his breath. My heart beats out what I don't want to say.

Goodbye.

20

SNIFFS AND WIGGLES

I LOOK UP at Kippy. He hops down a branch or two.

"He won't come?" Kippy asks.

I shake my head.

"Oh, Harvey, I'm so sorry," Kippy says.

"Me too." I look back at Chester. "But I understand."

"The French say it better," Chester tells me. "*Au revoir.* Until we meet again."

Chester's right, of course. That is better.

"We will meet again," I say. "I promise."

It's hard to leave him behind in the grove, but I've got to fix the promise I broke. The one to Danielle.

Kippy flies ahead, then back, and then around in anxious circles. We pass the small café again.

"Oh, dear," he says, flying ahead. "That was unexpected. All this way for naught."

Naught is a birdbrain way of saying *Nothing*.

"We came to find out if he needed help," I say. "Now we know he doesn't."

"Harvey! Harvey! Wait up for meeeeee!"

"Oh, my," Kippy says. "She's fast."

I turn to look and there's one of Chester's puppies, running, barking, tripping, and rolling.

"Wait up, wait up!"

It's the puppy with white-and-brown spots. Kippy's right. She is fast. And loud.

"Chester says you have a human for meeeeee!" She skids to a stop. "Hi, I'm Lila."

Kippy flies a little higher up into the sky.

"How do you do?" he calls down to her.

Lila tells us that Chester has sent her because she's ready to have a human.

"He knows I want one. And he says it's time for me to leave the sky," she says. "He says that I will grow up to be calm and good. But that I'm ready for a human now. Not like my brothers, who aren't ready. Not yet."

I look past her to the far edge of the café. I see Chester sitting there with three black-and-brown puppies. He nods at me. *Take her.* I look from them to Lila.

"I guess you're telling the truth," I say.

"Of course, I am!" Lila says. "Oh, my goodness, Harvey, I do not lie. But I know how to sit, be still, to poop and pee outside, bark at scary people, wag at good ones. I know so much!"

Lila thumps her tail back and forth, pleased as can be.

"Let's go, kid," I say.

And we do.

∾

I scratch and meow at Rachel's door.

"Should I bark?" Lila asks. "I have an excellent bark."

"No," I say. "No."

I'm nervous. Rachel said the last dog she loved was a calm, good soul. I know Lila is good. Chester would only raise a good dog.

But she is not calm yet.

The door opens and I see red pants. Very quickly, Lila's glossy, black fur is in my way.

She sniffs and wiggles. Her tail is everywhere.

"Oh, my goodness," Rachel says. "Oh, my goodness."

She crouches down and holds out her hand in a closed fist. She is very still as Lila sniffs her hand.

127

"How do you do, how do you do," Lila says. "You smell like the city after Christmas."

She is not quiet. She is not still.

"Look at you," Rachel says.

And here is this amazing thing: Rachel is QUIET. She is STILL.

It is the most I have ever liked her.

"You smell like so many yummy things," Lila tells her. "I could pee on you, but I won't because I'm good. How do you do, how do you do?"

"Are you a friend of Harvey's?" Rachel asks and her loud, annoying voice isn't loud or annoying.

"Chester sent me," Lila says.

"Harvey, I'm glad you're back," Rachel says to me in her normal voice.

It's loud and annoying.

"You'd better come inside," she says to Lila. "You need a bath and a meal."

She stands up and Lila squirms all around her legs. Those bright red pants are the perfect color for Lila's glossy black fur.

"What's a bath?" Lila says. "Is a meal food? I like food. Let's go!"

I watch them go inside. It's not exactly what I'd planned, but now Rachel has a dog, Lila has a human, and Chester has his place and his puppies.

I go up the stairs to my human, to ask her to forgive me.

CITY CREATURES

I MEOW AND scratch outside the door. I'm prepared to do it a lot. To do it until she lets me in. But after just one meow, Danielle opens the door.

"Oh, Harvey, I'm so glad you're here," she says. "I kept hoping you'd come right back."

And then she scoops me up and we sit together for a long time. I don't try to tell her where I've been or anything about Chester. She just rubs behind my ears and says *Kuh, tuk, kuk.*

She says it over and over until I fall asleep.

ఴ

Because I ran away, Danielle worries about my coming to the roof with her.

"Here's the thing," she says. "You're not my prisoner, but you are my cat."

I press my head into her hand. "You're my human," I tell her.

"And I want you to have some fresh air, but also be safe."

So, when we go to the roof, she picks me up and carries me up the stairs. I would so much rather walk, but I stay pressed into her arms. I smell her vanilla and mint smell and I listen to her quiet and gentle voice.

"If you run off a car might hit you or you could get lost," Danielle says. "Who knows what could happen?"

"I know what could happen," I tell her. "Big rats, angry cats, mean dogs, meaner humans."

Once we get to the roof, she shuts the door to the stairs and puts me down. I'm locked up on the roof with her. But I'm still free to wander around.

Danielle takes care of her plants, reads, or just sits. I smell the good dirt and feel the sun.

I say hello to the tower and the sky. They took care of me when I lived here and I don't forget that.

༄

Sometimes, I look out across the city and hope that everyone down there is as happy as I am. I always wonder what Chester and his young friends are up to in their grove in the park. When it's just Danielle and me, the sparrows come.

Swish, swish, swish.

They give me the news about my brother and sister. He still lives under the sky and she with her human. Both are safe and happy.

They say Chester found one of Lila's brothers a home, but the other two are still with him.

"They are problem cases," Flippy says, and I can tell those are Chester's words.

"Yes, yes, yes," says Mippy.

"Chester is good with problems," says Kippy.

Sometimes Rachel and Lila come up to the roof with us. The sparrows do not come when that happens. It's not restful for them.

Lila, like Rachel, is loud. At first, I think it's simply because she has moved so quickly from outside to inside. When I moved inside, I already knew Danielle. For Lila, both Rachel *and* the ceiling are new. Not to mention wet food, a leash, furniture, and her own bed.

"Harvey!" she yells every time she sees me. "I have so much to tell you!"

And then she wags her tail and barks out all her news.

But after a month or two, I realize that Lila is just loud. And like Rachel, she sometimes makes me want to hide under the bed. The time I actually do it, Lila wiggles in after me.

"Harvey, please come out," she says. "After Rachel and Chester, you're my favorite."

To be somebody's favorite is a nice thing. It really is. It's also nice to have a favorite.

"After Chester and Danielle, you're my favorite," I tell her, and I come out.

When she's at the apartment, I spend time with her, but not when we're all on the roof. There, Lila stays close to Rachel. She does not like to look out at the city.

"It makes me miss my brothers," she says. "And Chester."

But one day, she comes to stand near me. I listen to her breathing (which is loud) and smell her doggy smell. Rachel gives her a bath once a week, but Lila always smells like Lila—wet dirt and peanuts.

"Do you think my brothers are still in the park?" Lila asks. "The two without a human?"

"They are with Chester," I tell her. "They're safe."

"If I ran away to go and see them, could I find my way back?"

"Maybe," I say. "But you might not."

"But I might, right?" she asks. "Right, Harvey? I could, right?"

"Rachel would be so sad if you ran away," I say. "And so would you."

"She'd be happy when I came back, she would!" Lila says. "Do you think I would get lost? Really? Don't dogs always know how to get home? Don't they?"

"You don't need to see them badly enough to risk getting lost," I say.

"But I want to tell Chester and my brothers all about Rachel! I have so much to tell them," Lila barks out at me. "There are so many amazing things about Rachel. So many!"

I look over at Rachel, who is still loud with bright red pants and dark hair. But now I can see she is more than that. Rachel is kind and laughs easily. She loves both Lila and my human.

"You can ask Kippy to tell them all about her," I say. "He is good at delivering messages."

"I want to explain things *my* way," Lila says. "And touch my nose to their behinds."

Except for wanting to touch their behinds, I understand what it is Lila wants. She loves her life here, but like me, she misses life under the sky.

It's hard to go to the roof only when Danielle decides to take me with her. It's hard not to visit with Chester and the sparrows whenever I feel like it. It's hard to know I'll never again be a city cat living under the sky.

But then I look over at Danielle, who is planting and laughing with Rachel. If I never saw Danielle again, my heart would turn into a black, broken thing. I look from her to the city and back to Lila. The city is below us with the sky above.

I belong wherever these three creatures are. I am, as Chester said, attached. If Lila or any of them ran away or got hurt, I would go find them. I would face any danger at all—boys, sticks, humans, cranky cats, and crankier dogs—to find them.

That is all that's left on my list: To stay attached to the creatures and places I love. And if it's ever impossible to do that, I'm brave enough to find a way.

That's the kind of city cat I am: the Harvey kind.

ACKNOWLEDGMENTS

THE HUMANE RESCUE Alliance in Washington, DC, where I was a volunteer and met my cat (still ruling my house), showed me the good a city shelter provides. Richardson Rescue, in South Carolina, where I met my dog (RIP, Henry), first introduced me to volunteer-run rescue work. Tara Nicole Weyr, Deb Bloom, Louise Montgomery, and Barbara Davilman all taught me how to help animals without letting the overwhelming need for homes for the homeless ones drive me to despair. If you love animals and want to help them find homes, here are steps you can take: Adopt, never shop. Spay and neuter your pets. Foster (or ask your parents to foster) an animal in need. Donate time or money to a local rescue. You will literally save a life.

GARRET WEYR is the author of eight previous novels, including *The Language of Spells*, which had a dragon as its main character. She based his personality on her beloved rescue dog, Henry. She based Harvey's on a cat who followed her home, knowing she would help him. Her books have been banned, censored, and translated into over ten languages. She grew up in New York City, but she now lives in California with her animals—each of whom rescued her.

MINNIE PHAN is an illustrator based in Oakland, California. She is passionate about storytelling and inclusive image making. With a unique focus on diversity, her work ranges from editorial illustrations to comics, animation, and posters. When she isn't illustrating, she teaches comics to youth in the Bay Area; plays with her adopted bunny, Momo; and advocates for safer streets for bicyclists—and cats.